To Suz, the beekeeper

Illustrations copyright © 2011 by Craig Frazier

A Neal Porter Book
Published by Roaring Brook Press
Roaring Brook Press is a division of Holtzbrinck Publishing Holdings Limited Partnership
175 Fifth Avenue, New York, New York 10010
www.roaringbrookpress.com

Library of Congress Cataloging-in-Publication Data
Frazier, Craig, 1955–
  Bee & Bird / Craig Frazier. — 1st ed.
      p. cm.
  "A Neal Porter book."
  Summary: In this wordless picture book, a bumblebee and a bird embark on a travel adventure.
  ISBN 978-1-59643-660-2
  [1. Bumblebees—Fiction. 2. Birds—Fiction. 3. Travel—Fiction. 4. Adventure and adventurers—Fiction.
5. Stories without words.] I. Title. II. Title: Bee and Bird.
  PZ7.F869Be 2011
  [E]—dc22
                                                                        2010013012

Roaring Brook Press books are available for special promotions and premiums.
For details contact: Director of Special Markets, Holtzbrinck Publishers.

First Edition 2011
Book design by Craig Frazier
Printed in January 2011 in China by South China Printing Co. Ltd., Dongguan City, Guangdong Province

10 9 8 7 6 5 4 3 2 1

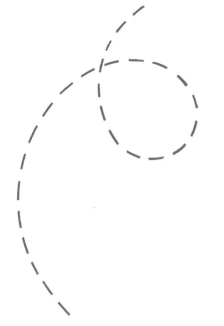

Bee&Bird

Craig Frazier

A NEAL PORTER BOOK

ROARING BROOK PRESS

NEW YORK

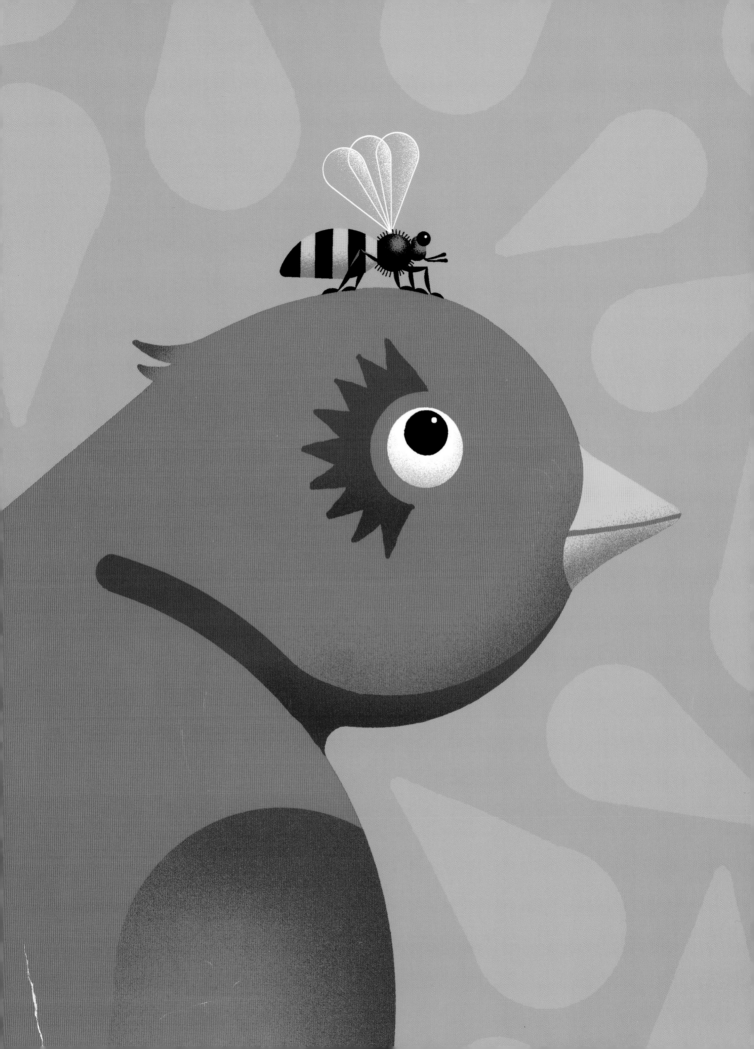

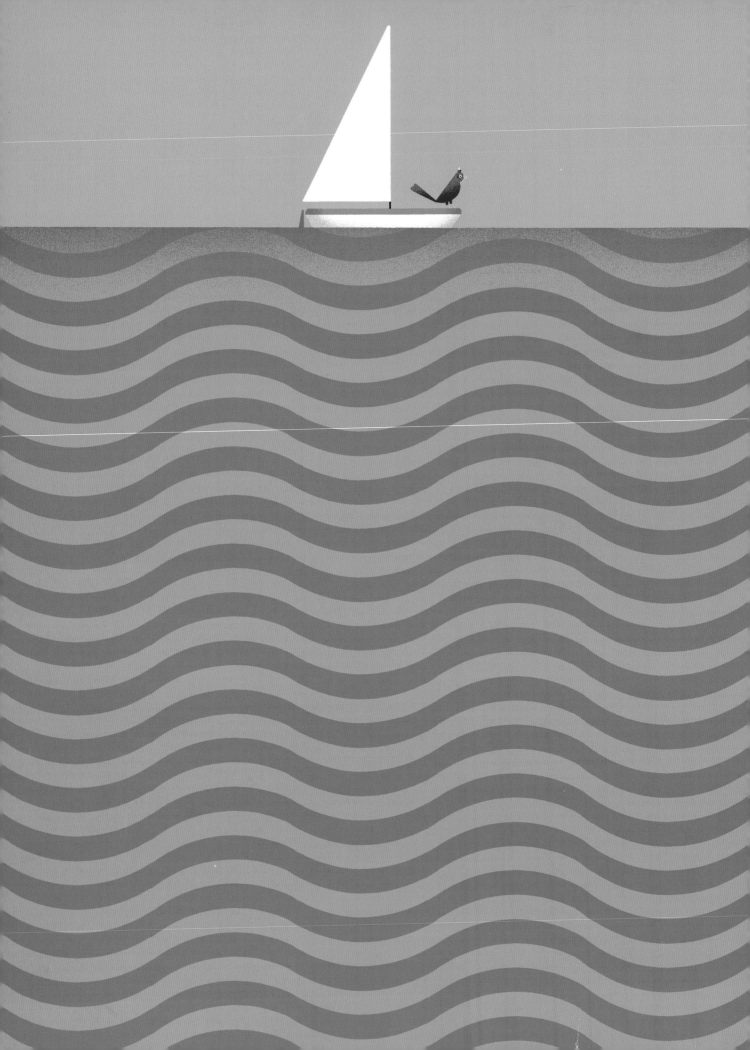

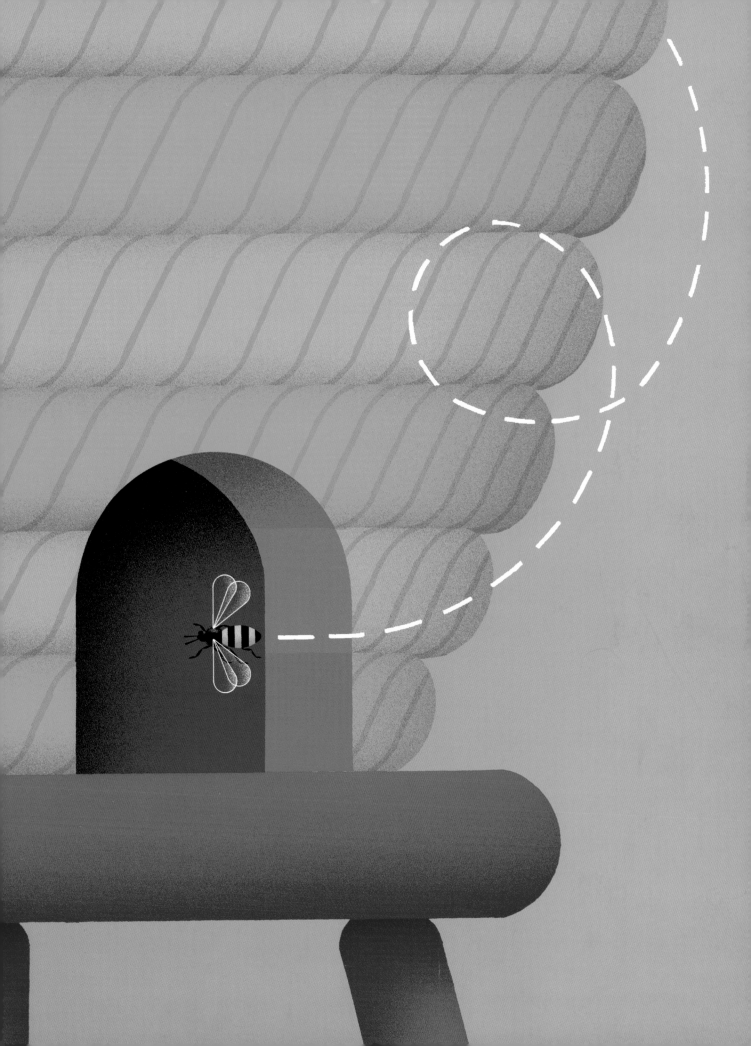

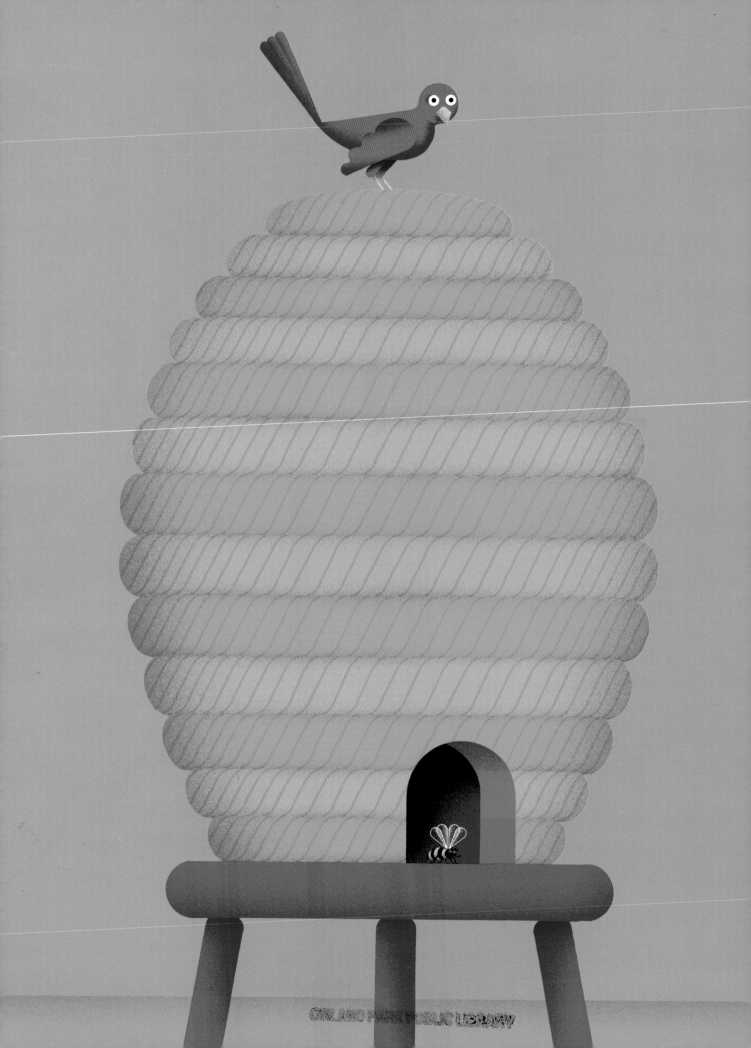